June 3, 2022

Author: Jerry Juergens

&

Illustrator:

A Star Named Twinkle

ARTIST
And
Illustrator

Jerry E. Juergens

A Children's Story of Hope

First published by AuthorHouse 11/02/04

ISBN: 1-4184-8682-5 (sc)

Library of Congress Control Number: 2004097200

Printed in the United States of America
Bloomington, Indiana

This book is printed on acid-free paper.

authorHOUSE

1663 LIBERTY DRIVE
BLOOMINGTON, INDIANA 47403
(800) 839-8640
www.authorhouse.com

About the Author

Jerry Juergens was born in Huntington Indiana. Jerry has a twin brother George, who both became Eagle Boy Scouts,the top award The Boy Scout of America hands out. They would lead scouts in songs on all their outings. Jerry loved to tell bedtime stories.

Jerry married his wife Mary, and they have been married for 47 years. Together they were youth counselors at their church for over ten years, and again Jerry would tell them bedtime stories.

Jerry and his wife Mary winter in Lake Region, Florida. Jerry is an artist and is in several art shows both in Florida and Indiana. He is in excellent health and in his youth set several track records.

Before he retired he Designed and built homes for over 12 years, and also worked with his father and brother operating Juergens hardware store before he went into the Insurance business where he received several top company awards.

He and his wife have two sons, Perry and Curt and between all four they strive to reach their goals and this book is dedicated to them and that cause.

All the billions of stars in the sky And God picked Twinkle
to be the Star of Bethlehem.

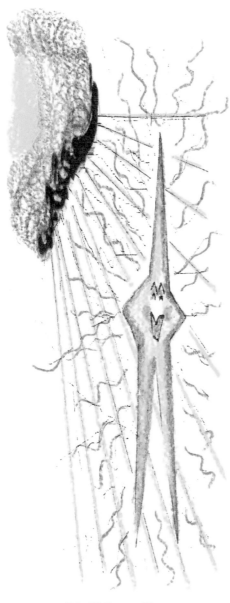

This is a story
of hope.
For children that
think they are small
in whatever thoughts
they
might have.
Way back in B.C. the
'Star Of Bethlehem'
was sighted.

From where did the
star come?

How did it develop?

Why did our creator
pick this particular
star to lead the
shepherds to
baby Jesus?

Read the story!

PREFACE

Twinkle was a star among billions of other stars in the heavens. Unlike many of his fellow star friends, he was very lonely because he was so small. His friends were bigger, they had important jobs to do and they also lived in famous places like the LITTLE DIPPER, the BIG DIPPER, and the MILKY WAY. Twinkle thought he was just too small to be important.

Since Twinkle was born such a little star, he would always dream about what it would be like to be big and important. He would dream about what it would be like to live in the famous Milky Way. Although the Milky Way would be too crowded. It was still better than where Twinkle was living all by himself. He thought he was a star that no one wanted.

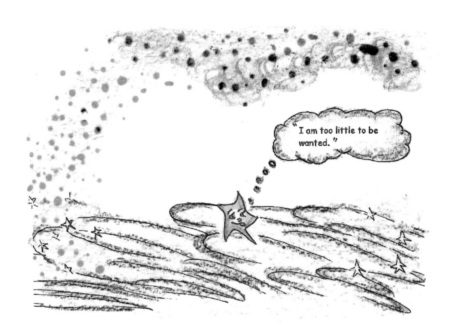

Twinkle would dream about the famous Big Dipper. All the people on earth are always looking for the Big Dipper. Those stars are always so easy to find and it makes the people on earth so happy and proud of themselves when they find them. Twinkle thought to himself, "I would be so proud if just one of the stars of the Big Dipper would move over and make room for me. I wouldn't take up much room. I'm such a little star. I sure would be grateful.

Twinkle was positive this would never happen. Twinkle was sure he didn't stand a chance, asking the Big Dipper if he could join their group. So Twinkle went to ask the Little Dipper.

Twinkle thought they would be more his size, since they were in the Little Dipper.

Twinkle was very surprised to see that they also were very big stars. They thought they were so important, and so smart. [They even made fun of Little Twinkle.] They made him feel bad. They said things like: They had no room for such a little spark like him. The spoke person for the Little Dipper said, "This is a special group and we don't let just any heavenly body enter. Especially little sparks like you."

When Twinkle would feel bad he would always go to his creator and ask for help. God is so proud of his creations. God wants everybody to be happy. The Great Creator is always coming up with something especially in order to help his creation of mankind. For instance, God created man to have dominion over the fish of the sea, and over the birds in the air, and over the cattle, and over all the earth. Then God decided it was not good for man to be alone, so God created woman.

In the year 4 b. c. God decided to have a son with Mary, and she would name him Jesus, for he will save his people from their sins.

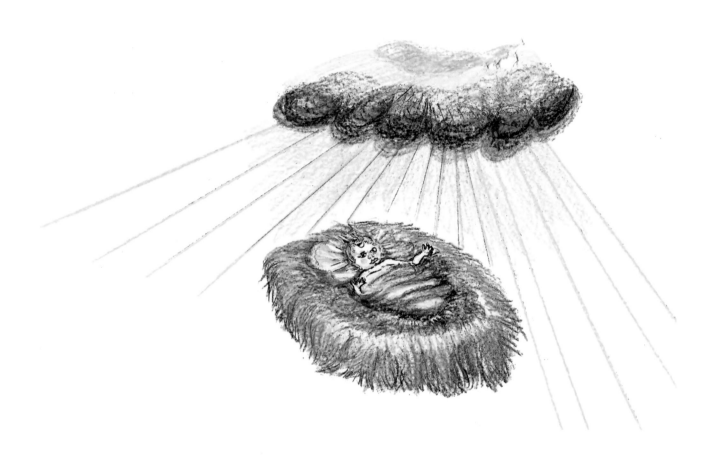

God wanted a star to lead the Wise men to find Baby Jesus. These men were a wide variety of people, including fortune-tellers, priestly magicians, and astrologers. They came from afar, such as Babylonia and Persia. God wanted the finest of all the stars to lead these men to Baby Jesus. The star that shines the prettiest, and is the most unique will be the star, "The Star Of Bethlehem!" So God decided to have a contest.

Little Twinkle became very excited when he heard the news of the contest. He thought to himself, "If I work real hard, I could be that star. I could really be a famous star!"
Twinkle went from star to star to see if they would help him win the contest. They too were also interested in winning the contest, and would not help Little Twinkle.

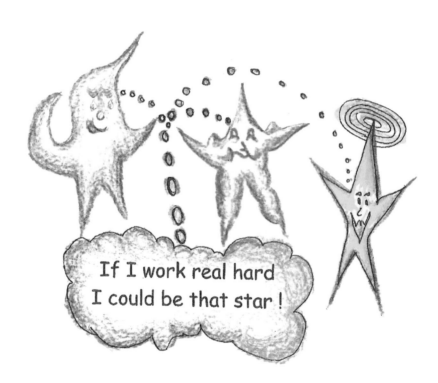

So Little Twinkle decided to exercise and practice. Twinkle believed the more he would exercise and practice the bigger and more beautiful he would become.

After a long time of working out went by, he started to notice something was happening. He kept on working out, but he also concentrated on what was happening around him. Then he saw it! The more he would spin around, the more stardust his body would throw off. This made him look big and beautiful. Now he sparkled! The little star was very excited about this trick he was capable of doing. He also was aware that just maybe other stars could also do this same trick. In order to become the best at this trick he would have to practice harder and exercise more. So he could be the best.

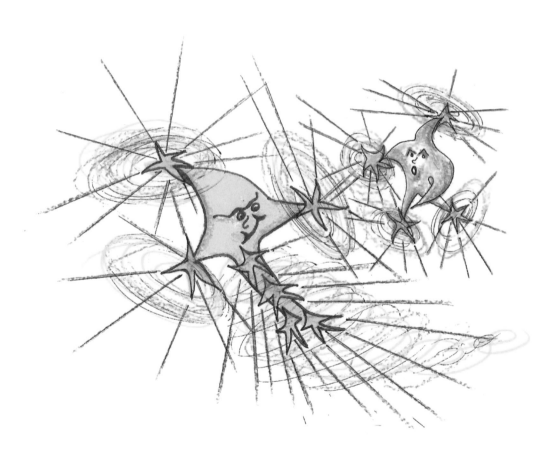

Most stars are only a mass of light. Some have five points, and some have four points. Now Little Twinkle had two points on each side. Then, for a beautiful accent he had sparkling stardust shooting high above him, and a long sparkling stardust drifting far below him. Little Twinkle was so proud of himself, that he wanted to practice more and more all the time.

Twinkle knew if he didn't win the contest, he would still be proud of himself for discovering what all he could do. He knew the contest would be fair and there would be lots of stars competing in this contest. After all, they are going to have ideas, also.

Little Twinkle was satisfied with everything that he had accomplished.

The contest was now ready to start! All the contestants were called upon to do their best on why they think they should be picked to be the Star of Bethlehem.

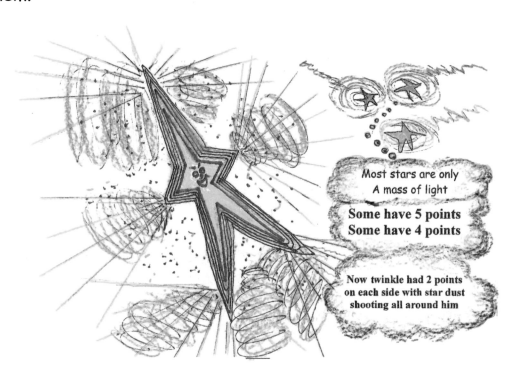

The first stars to start the contest was the big mass of fireball stars, which would shine and throb. They were something to behold. Next was the four pointed stars. They stretched out as far as t hey could, making sure their points were sharp and pointed as they could be. They also looked great. Then came the big fancy five-pointed stars, also making sure their points were sharp and stretched out as far as they could possibly stretch them, so they could look big and beautiful.

God looked them all over and studied them very closely. Little Twinkle was waiting for God to look over most of the stars before he went into his routine. Twinkle was surprised when he noticed that he was the only star that worked up a routine. Twinkle also realized from the very beginning of the contest that he had to conserve his energy, until he was ready to be judged.

While God was inspecting the other stars, Twinkle rested.

GOD LOOKED THEM OVER VERY CLOSELY

The other stars, waiting to be judged, were snickering at Little Twinkle. "What are you doing here?" "Grow up!" "This is for big, beautiful stars like us!" "What can you do?"
Little Twinkle would just keep quiet, thinking all the time. "This is going to be so good." Twinkle worked so hard for this moment. All the other stars had to do was to show up, no working, no practicing, or anything.

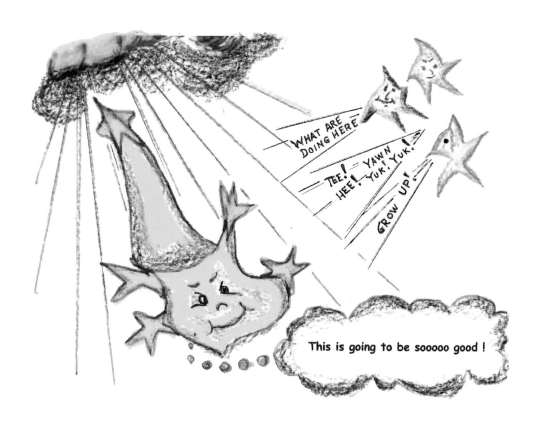

God was almost finished and was just getting ready to look at Twinkle when all of a sudden Little Twinkle went into his routine. He started spinning and rubbing his top points together and throwing the sparkling stardust as high as he could. At the same time he started rubbing his bottom points together and letting the sparking stardust drift far below him! It was so awesome that all the stars in the heavens started dancing and shooting across the sky like never before recorded in Solar history.

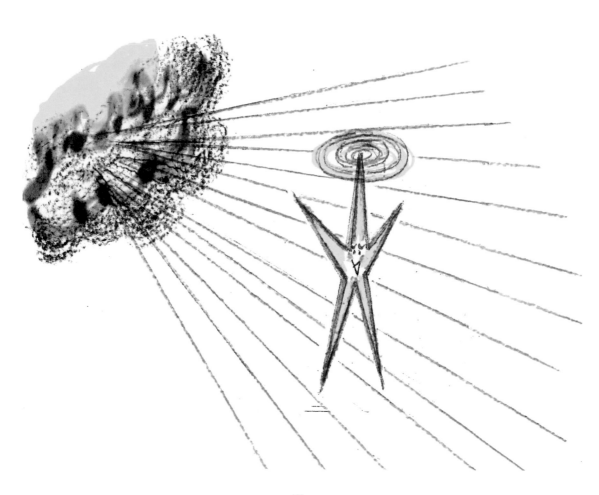

God was so pleased. God knew in the very beginning that Twinkle was going to be the winner if Twinkle was willing to work hard and not give up. God spoke to Twinkle. "This was exactly what I was looking for, Little Twinkle, you are the Star Of The East—THE STAR OF BETHLEHEM!"

All the other stars in the heavens came around and congratulated Twinkle for a job well done.

Twinkle learned a good lesson. It pays to work hard.

Believe in your goals, and do not let anyone talk you out of them. The most important thing of all is, do not forget to say your prayers, and think like a star.

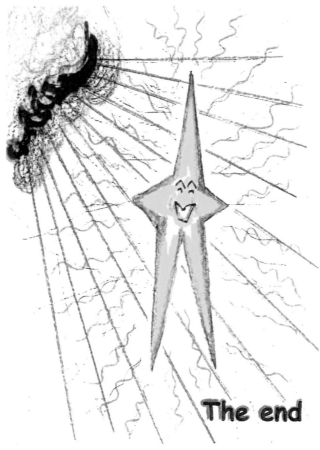

The end

Made in United States
Orlando, FL
06 December 2022